MARKED MATE

INTERSTELLAR BRIDES® PROGRAM
BOOK 24

GRACE GOODWIN

Marked Mate
Copyright © 2023 by TydByts Media

This book was written by a human and not Artificial Intelligence (A.I.).

This book may not be used to train Artificial Intelligence (A.I.).

Interstellar Brides® is a registered trademark .

All Rights Reserved. No part of this book may be reproduced or transmitted in any form or by any means, electrical, digital or mechanical including but not limited to photocopying, recording, scanning or by any type of data storage and retrieval system without express, written permission from the author.

Published by TydByts Media
Goodwin, Grace
Cover design copyright 2022 by TydByts Media
Images/Photo Credit: Deposit Photos: frenta; diversepixel; Angela_Harburn; ferrerivideo;

Publisher's Note:
This book was written for an adult audience. The book may contain explicit sexual content. Sexual activities included in this book are strictly fantasies intended for adults and any activities or risks taken by fictional characters within the story are neither endorsed nor encouraged by the author or publisher.

SUBSCRIBE TODAY!

PATREON

*H*i there! Grace Goodwin here. I am SO excited to invite you into my intense, crazy, sexy, romantic, imagination and the worlds born as a result. From Battlegroup Karter to The Colony and on behalf of the entire Coalition Fleet of Planets, I welcome you! Visit my Patreon page for additional bonus content, sneak peaks, and insider information on upcoming books as well as the opportunity to receive NEW RELEASE BOOKS before anyone else! See you there! ~ Grace

Grace's PATREON: https://www.patreon.com/gracegoodwin

GET A FREE BOOK!

JOIN MY MAILING LIST TO STAY INFORMED OF NEW RELEASES, FREE BOOKS, SPECIAL PRICES AND OTHER AUTHOR GIVEAWAYS.

http://freescifiromance.com

FIND YOUR INTERSTELLAR MATCH!

YOUR mate is out there. Take the test today and discover your perfect match. Are you ready for a sexy alien mate (or two)?

VOLUNTEER NOW!
interstellarbridesprogram.com

1

Elite Hunter Stark, Earth Landing Site, Cleveland, Ohio

Not now.

Not again.

A wave of dizziness forced me to plant my palm against the wall of my ship for balance. For the last few hours, as I'd scouted this planet for the criminals I hunted, something had been assaulting my senses. Something I'd never felt before. Intense. Confusing. Without source or reason. I would have suspected a pathogen on the planet if the illness hadn't begun while I had been in orbit.

I had no explanation or theory behind what might be wrong with me. I'd used my ReGen wand to run a full health assessment as soon as I'd landed. According to the annoyingly bright, little blue-green lights, I was in perfect health—

"Fu—" Pain exploded inside my skull with the force of a dagger's strike. Heat raced over my skin in a wave. My palm burned. My stomach heaved. My cock grew hard and achy, desperate to find release. Desperate to find...*her?*

What. The. Fuck?

The ReGen wand had to be malfunctioning. I'd go to medical as soon as I completed this mission.

"Get it together, Stark." I used a severe tone when I issued the command to myself. I couldn't afford weakness. Some of the most vile, evil criminals ever born had escaped the Everian prison ship—with the help of their fellow Siren Legion operatives from Rogue 5. My fellow Hunters had been tasked with finding the accomplices. I'd been sent here to hunt the Siren scum who had set up shop on this primitive, backward planet.

The people of Earth were, according to my research, the newest members of the Interstellar Coalition of Planets. Earth was well known for its lack of...a lot of things. The humans here still fought wars over resources and territory. They allowed their own people to starve and were trapped in a monetary system designed to ensure the wealthy remained so while the majority of their people struggled daily to obtain basic necessities. The Coalition protected the people of Earth, but did not trust them. Not yet. Perhaps in a couple hundred years.

In fact, I hadn't understood why Earth had been allowed into the Coalition until I saw a bride from Earth at the Touchstone. My friend, Zee, had claimed a human female for his mate. More, she was his marked mate, a perfect match, their souls capable of a connection both rare and revered by all people from Everis. I harbored no belief that such a female existed for me. That was for the best as I had no time for a mate. There was always evil to hunt.

I rubbed my brow as the pain lessened and adjusted my painfully engorged cock in my armor. Was this a psychic attack? There was no other explanation. I had trained for years to perfect my mental defenses. Had the criminals from Rogue 5 managed to modify the tech in a Prillons' mating collars to create a new telepathic weapon?

I walked down the ramp and activated the security system. The ship's cloaking tech responded to a flick of my wrist. The ship silently floated up to hover above the building's fourth story roof. Once it was in place, the sleek black vessel disappeared before my eyes.

The onboard sensors would adjust the altitude to keep the ship out of reach, should any humans stumble their way onto the roof. I wouldn't be long. I'd tracked my prey to this city. I was an Elite Hunter. One of the best.

Finding the three Siren operatives and bringing them to justice would be simple. I would be on my way back to Everis in a matter of hours.

Hot, muggy air settled on me like a damp blanket. Another flood of heat swamped my system and my cock throbbed, my vision blurred. With renewed ferocity, something or someone battered the walls I'd built around my mind with a psychic hammer.

Gritting my teeth, I forced my surroundings into tight focus and sent my instincts out, looking for a direction, a hint of movement, for the enemy presence here.

There. Siren scum. I had what I needed.

A target.

Rebecca, *Miami, Florida, Earth*

This was stupid. Insane. Was I really this eager to get myself killed the day before I was supposed to start my new life?

I didn't turn around and hurry home at the thought, so, yes. Guess I was. Because I had to help those kids and it was now or never. In twenty-four hours this town wouldn't be my home anymore. I was leaving tomorrow. Moving truck would arrive first thing in the morning. Then I had some paperwork to drop off at the youth center. I'd already spent the last six months training my replacements. I'd been accepted to the college program that was first on my list. Class started in less than two weeks. Everything was arranged. I was going to get my degree so I could make more of a difference. Recruit sponsors. Expand the center. Offer therapy and some basic health care to kids for whom the youth center was their second home.

I'd been stuck in this rut long enough.

Stopping to carefully peek into the next dark alley, I sighed as the darkness hovered on the edges of the space, barely held at bay by dirty, yellowed street lights and the reflection of the full moon in water puddles that dotted the cracked stretch of pavement. The raging headache I'd had for the last few hours hadn't improved my mood. Nothing would. Nothing but stopping the jerks who had hurt Andreas. He was only fifteen. Too young for this bullshit.

His home life had finally begun to improve. He had a new foster family who adored him. He was doing better in school. I'd actually seen him *smile* the last couple weeks.

And now this?

Squatting next to my Bull Mastiff, Lilah, I laid my arm over her back and listened for voices coming from the alley. Footsteps. Anything that would indicate a person was near.

Nothing. The dark stretch of shadows between buildings smelled like dirty car oil, burned tires and urine—that last courtesy of the bar patrons inside the brick building next to me.

Lilah snorted and tried to lick my face with her enormous tongue. Not my nose or cheek, my entire face. She weighed almost two hundred pounds, had silky golden fur, a black face and the saddest eyes I'd ever seen. I didn't know how such a huge creature could throw such pathetic puppy eyes at me when she wanted something, but she did. And I gave in. Every time.

"Let's go, girl." I slipped around the corner with Lilah right behind me, the perfect amount of slack in her leash. I'd worked with her since she was a puppy, making sure that when she grew up, she knew how to behave. I loved big dogs but I also knew they could be a lot to handle if you didn't start training them young.

She padded along at my side as I carefully placed

each step, determined not to make a sound. I had always been able to move quietly, scaring friends and family on multiple occasions; a talent I appreciated now. My plan was to locate where these bastards had set up their operation, and turn them in to the police. If they saw me, I had the perfect excuse to be outside. I was just a simple girl from the neighborhood out walking her dog. I would find them. The police would round them up, and my kids would be safe. Well, not safe—no one was ever completely safe in this part of town—but *safer*.

My cell phone buzzed in my back pocket and I pulled it out to check the text. It was from one of my co-workers at the youth center.

A<small>NDREAS IS OK</small>. *Doc sending him home.*

M<small>Y HAND SHOOK</small> as I responded with a simple *thank you* and put my phone away. The birthmark on my palm itched. *Again*. The darn thing had been driving me crazy all day. I rubbed my hand along the seam of my jeans to ease the burn and kept walking. I was close. I could feel it.

I knew the men I sought were pure evil. They had to be. No one else could distribute that kind of drug to kids.

To *my kids*. Teens who came to me for safety and shelter, who told me about the hellish lives they led at home or about how often they went hungry. I loved these kids. Watched over them. I was like a savage older sister with an unforgiving attitude. No one messed with my kids.

These alien assholes had put one of them in the hospital this afternoon with their new, designer drug. They called it 'Quell'. No one had ever heard of it before a few weeks ago. Not my contact at the police station or the kids I knew who kept dangerous—*gangster*—company. No one had heard of this particular gang before either. They had appeared out of nowhere, started selling the drug and killing any other gangs or drug dealers who stood in their way.

They were efficient, I'd give them that. The police had their hands full processing dead bodies. I'd read on a local news feed the FBI and DEA had been called in to help stop the violence. Our city was being destroyed by a '*gang war*'.

True, my city wasn't Beverly Hills, but it was home and now it was turning into a freaking disaster. No one could get close to the new dealers. It was like they could read minds or something. They never got caught; always got away.

But Andreas had whispered something to me before he collapsed, slipping unconscious as the paramedics loaded him into the back of their ambulance.

Aliens.

I'd asked who sold him the Quell, where he got his hands on it, and that was the only word he'd spoken. Aliens. God damn, freaking aliens.

And then he'd pressed his hoodie into my hands with a terrified look on his face. He took my hand and wrapped it around something about the size of my fist that he had hidden in the pocket and said, '*Its theirs. I stole it. I'm sorry. They'll come for it. I'm so sorry.*'

He'd sobbed like a three year old. I'd asked what it was and why he'd taken it. How this had happened. Who had given him the drug. I spoke so quickly the words slurred together. No that it mattered. He'd had one more word for me – *aliens*—then he'd passed out while I rambled. The first responders lifted him into their van, slammed the doors in my face and drove away.

A few years ago I would have laughed at the idea of aliens like everyone else. But one of my best friends, Katie, had volunteered to be an Interstellar Bride. She'd walked into that processing center and never come back out. The aliens had some kind of transporter, *Beam-me-up-Scotty,* technology in that building. I'd received the money she'd been awarded for volunteering and a note telling me she was tired of Earth and all the crazy. She wanted a fresh start.

Her parents both being drug addicts as well as dealers, I didn't blame her one bit. I'd used the money to improve the center and to pay Lilah's rescue fee. She'd been the best birthday present I'd ever given myself. A puppy. A clumsy, adorable puppy with the biggest feet I'd ever seen.

And now I was out at night in a scary part of town, lurking in dark alleys. Did I have a gun? A knife? Even pepper spray? How about a Jedi Knight to protect me with his bright blue light saber? Big *NOPE* to all of those. I had a dog. A great big, lick my face every chance she got, two hundred pound lap dog. She made me feel safer. Right now, that was all that mattered.

Ten minutes and two turns later I stood across the street from a run-down strip mall. Once upon a time this had been a bright and shiny shopping center. Now the bricks crumbled on every corner, several windows were boarded up where the glass had broken and no one cared enough to fix it, and the parking lot was more potholes than pavement.

There was a light on inside the defunct business on the end. The retail space was not huge, but it had a drive up window where, right now, a dark SUV pulled up and rolled down the driver's side window.

A low rumble came from Lilah. A growl. A warning.

"Shhh, girl." I took out my cell phone so I could take a picture of the license plate. I zoomed in and out, trying to bring the numbers and letters into focus. "Got it." I hit the button to take the picture.

Bright light flashed from my phone. The SUV's reverse lights came on and it backed up toward me as a couple of huge men came out the front door of the business.

The SUV skidded to a halt. I saw a flash. Heard a loud crack.

"Shit."

I looked down to see a dark stain blossoming on my side, soaking my favorite yellow blouse.

The SUV sped away. The two huge men were menacing shadows now, quickly closing in on me.

Lilah stepped between us and bared her teeth, a deep warning growl directed at the two shadows. They stopped about ten paces from me, wary but not scared.

"What are you doing here, female?" The voice was harsh. Unforgiving.

"Walking---my dog." I pressed my palm to my side,

felt the warm blood and then lifted my fingers in front of my face to confirm what I suspected. Dark red stained my fingers and palm. The ground started to spin. Instinctively, I put my hand on Lilah's back to steady myself.

The second shadow spoke, his voice more of a growl. Deeper. Cruel. "We don't have time for this. We need to find the key." He stared at me, his smile cruel.

Shit. Did he have *fangs?*

"Let her bleed out. Kill the animal. We will dump the bodies later."

The first man followed orders. He lifted his arm in my direction, pointing his gun at Lilah. Not a normal gun. A strange, silver space gun.

These were the definitely the aliens. I'd found them.

Hysterical laughter bubbled up inside me; I knew I was dying. But these assholes were not going to kill my dog. "No!"

I threw myself in front of Lilah as a bolt of light came from the end of his weapon. Fiery pain exploded in my hip as my opposite shoulder slammed into concrete. My skull hit next, the pain causing black spots at the edges of my vision, quickly forming a tunnel as I tried to stay conscious.

"Don't hurt her." I lifted my hand, palm out in an appeal. "Don't. Please."

A shadow appeared behind the two assailants. Darker. Silent. Like Death himself coming for me.

Scalding heat exploded though my hand, a welcome distraction from the pain.

Except, I didn't hurt anymore. I didn't feel anything...

The dark shadow moved closer, coming up behind

the two aliens. The faint light of a distant streetlamp illuminated his features. Chiseled jaw. Dark eyes. Black hair. Lips that were pure sin. He was beautiful. So very beautiful. Death was supposed to be an angel, too? Wasn't he?

If *that* was the angel of Death, he could take me. Hopefully more than once.

Lilah barked, pulling at her leash. I didn't have the strength to hold her back. I thought I heard shouts over her loud growling, but the sounds were far away. The hard concrete pressed painfully into my bones. My head throbbed. Cold. I was cold now. So cold. Everywhere except my hand. That was warm. So nice. So warm.

So tired.

I closed my eyes and imagined my angel of Death holding me, telling me everything was going to be all right. I held onto the fantasy as long as I could, until there was nothing at all.

2

WHAT WAS the human doing here? No sane female would seek out these bastards.

Until she appeared, everything had been going to plan. Humans in a black vehicle had arrived to pick up some Quell at the odd window on the side of the building. I'd marked their vehicle so I could track them once I was done here.

Then? Chaos. Human weapons firing. The female was injured, severely.

The Siren operatives didn't know I was here. Not yet. But I would take pleasure in ending their lives. Males of worth did not harm females of any species.

"Let her bleed out. Kill the animal. We can dump the bodies later."

I moved closer without making a sound.

"No!" The female's voice rang out.

I watched the Rogue 5 hybrid lift his ion blaster and point it toward the animal. I could not afford to intervene. Rokor, their leader, was dangerous. Deadly. I could not lose foc—

I felt the blast to my hip as if I were the one shot. The barrier in my mind shattered like broken glass and suddenly I was seeing through two sets of eyes.

She held up her small, blood-stained hand and begged for her pet's life. "Don't hurt her. Don't. Please."

I saw myself through her eyes, a shadow moving closer, Death himself. She was not afraid of dying, nor of me. She wanted—*Fuck.* My cock twitched. Hard. Hot. My hand burned. She wanted to be in my arms. She ached for me.

She was *mine*.

The connection faded yet I clung to the fleeting warmth in my mind, desperate to feel it again. It had only been a few seconds, but I was out of time.

Her beast must have sensed the danger as well. The golden animal charged the male who held the ion blaster. The smell of burning flesh filled the air as the beast was shot, but it did not stop. It leaped, its weight making the male stagger and fall. Her pet rushed in for the kill, its huge black maw on the male's neck.

I was there instantly, my blaster at the male's temple. I ended his struggle and rose to take care of their leader.

Rokor turned to assist his partner, found me instead. He raised his hands above his head. He didn't run, he dropped his chin in a mockery of a bow.

I wanted him to run. I wanted to chase him down

before I killed him. He was responsible for gravely injuring my female. Had ordered her death with no emotion nor remorse. His smirk held no remorse. No fear. He glanced down at the insignia on my uniform, just below my shoulder.

"An Elite Hunter? I wasn't aware that I was of such interest to the Coalition Fleet."

Disgust bubbled within me, but I did not linger on the feeling. My mate needed me. I did not have time to argue with this evil bastard. "Dead or alive. Your choice."

"Alive."

"When will your third be back?" Three of them had escaped the prison. They were all here, on Earth. I could *feel* them. Two here. One...not far. An easy hunt.

He smiled at me. Fucking smiled. Then he turned his hand enough for me to see the transport beacon he held.

I fired. Too late. He was gone.

A jolt of heat flashed through my palm, shocking me back to the present. To *her*.

I ran to her and knelt at her side, my pulse racing, not from the short fight but from being close to her. The scent of her skin wrapped around me, some kind of flower, no doubt. One I did not recognize, though it managed to seduce me all the same. I reached for her head where I saw blood matting her dark hair. I did not get close before her beast growled a warning.

"I'm not going to hurt her. I promise."

The animal sniffed at me with a cold, wet nose, her black face and dark eyes focused on me with a surprising amount of intelligence. I took that for permission to continue and immediately returned my attention to the unconscious female. My female.

Using what medical supplies I had with me, I managed to stop the bleeding. But the items I carried were minimal, sufficient for emergencies only. They would help someone injured survive long enough to get back to their ship or a doctor. My mate needed more than this. She needed a ReGen pod. Blood. Days to heal. Most importantly, she needed to refrain from placing herself in danger, from chasing treacherous criminals.

She needed me.

Moving quickly I settled her back to the ground, her furry protector laying along her other side, watchful but calm. I took a DNA sample from the corpse of the dead criminal to confirm my kill. Stripping him of his weapons took mere seconds. I placed a bioflare on the corpse and activated it. Within minutes the body would be gone, burned to dust and ash. The human authorities did not need an alien body, potentially filled with illegal Hive tech, to dissect.

I returned to my mate and nearly forgot to breathe. She was uncommonly beautiful with warm, brown skin, softer than any I had ever touched. Black hair, wild with curls, surrounded her face, and her lips were full and ripe for kissing. I shuddered as I imagined tasting those lips. Having them wrapped around my hard length.

With professional efficiency, I checked for any additional wounds, placing a pressure bandage over the angry hole just below her ribs.. Her body was neither small nor frail. Full hips. Large breasts. Soft thighs. I would melt into her softness. She would feel like home. Like peace.

I turned her hand, palm up and my heart staggered when I saw the mark there. This was not a trick of my mind. Somehow, she was truly mine. My marked mate.

She was magnificent.

Turning to her beast, I reached for the patch of burned hair and flesh on the creature's shoulder. Another soft growl of warning and I decided to leave the wound, for now. The animal did not seem to be in pain. More importantly, it clearly did not wish to be touched. At least, not by me. I had done what I could for my mate's pet. Clearly the creature meant a lot to her. Enough to throw her body in front of an ion blast.

"Damn female. You are not to do that again." My attempt to scold her failed completely, my reprimand much softer than it should have been.

I lifted her into my arms and reveled in her softness pressed to me. As I carried her back to my ship, her beast walked next to me. I wasn't sure whether the creature's intention was to watch over my mate or to keep me in line.

Protective. I approved.

The hunt would have to wait. I had more important things to do. Heal her. Claim her. Bring her pleasure.

I had not imagined myself with a marked mate, yet now that I held her I knew I could never let her go. I would do whatever was necessary to woo her, to make her truly mine.

3

ebecca, Medical Station, Stark's Ship

WARMTH ROSE FROM A SOFT, comfortable surface beneath me. Lying on my back I stretched just a bit, pointed my toes and inhaled deeply. The air smelled odd. In fact, it didn't smell like anything. No gasoline fumes, pizza ovens or trash.

Where the hell was I?

I opened my eyes.

Shit. I was in a coffin. A glass coffin like freaking Snow White in the woods. Except no handsome prince was coming to kiss me and make everything better.

Was I dead? Was this a dream?

I looked down at my body and discovered I was naked. Totally. Completely. Bare-ass naked.

I had to be dead. What happened to me? Recent events struggled through the fog in my head. Andreas.

He'd given me his jacket with the strange, glowing thing. I'd gone to the youth center, put it in my fire-proof safe and grabbed Lilah's leash to take a walk. I'd found the drug dealers who---

"Oh, shit." Aliens. Where were those two huge aliens that shot me?

And the guys in that black SUV? They'd shot me first, with a very human bullet. Then the space laser. They were going to kill my dog. And me. And *'dump the bodies'*.

"Lilah." Had she escaped? Run away? Had that jerk with freaking *fangs* killed her after I lost consciousness? I hoped she had run back to the youth center. There was almost always someone around, and they all knew my great big snuggle-bug of a dog. Lilah was probably with the kids right now, head resting in one of their laps, basking in all the attention.

I ran my hand over my abdomen and hip, searching for the wounds I knew were there. Nothing but smooth skin. No blood. No pain.

Well fine. Definitely dead then.

Highly disappointing; I wasn't done living yet.

I wiped the tears from my eyes and studied the translucent shell covering me from head to toe. Dead or not, I wasn't staying inside a glass coffin. And I was going to find some clothes.

Palms out, I pushed up. Tried to lift the damn thing.

"Good God." The heavy lid didn't budge. Didn't vibrate. Nothing.

Good thing I liked leg press on the rare occasion I went to the gym. I didn't have little nothing, skinny girl thighs. Not me. They were big and round. Might be soft on the outside, but inside? Pure power. I pulled my knees up toward my chest until I could get the bottoms of my feet flat against the glass and pushed. Hard.

"Giiirl poweeeer." Inhale. Pause. Exhale, push harder.

A distinct pop encouraged me to continue. It was breaking.

A crack appeared under my heel.

"Yes!" Two cracks. Splinters of shattering glass appeared and spread down the sides. I closed my eyes and wrapped my arms around my head to protect my face. This coffin was going to blow and I didn't need a thousand cuts or glass in my eyes. The rest of me? I'd deal with that once I was out of this freaking *coffin*.

"Stop! What are you doing?" A deep male voice shouted the words but he sounded like he was yelling at me underwater in a swimming pool. Muffled. Distant.

My right foot thrust forward as the glass gave way under my heel. Searing pain burned through me as the jagged edges of the cover shredded my ankle and lower leg.

Wincing, I pulled my foot back inside and chose a new placement right next to the hole I had created.

I didn't care how many times I had to shove my leg through, how many cuts I would have. I was going to make a hole big enough to crawl out no matter what it cost me.

Being buried alive in a glass coffin was not okay. Nowhere near okay. I had mild claustrophobia. Most of the time it didn't bother me.

Right now? Right now, I was willing to do whatever I had to do to get the hell out of this tiny box.

Crossing my arms over my face once more, I pushed with my legs again.

Splinters. Cracks. The distinct popping and crackling noises encouraged me to—

The glass was gone and my feet were sticking up, free in mid-air. What the--?

"By the gods, female! What are you doing? Trying to kill yourself? I just managed to make you healthy again!"

Rolling my head in the direction the voice came from, I lowered my arms to cover my bare breasts and blinked to clear the fog from my vision. I felt the hot blood rolling down my leg like rain sliding down a windowpane, but I didn't dare look. I lowered my feet so they were flat on the pad I was lying on and stared.

Holy shit. I had to be dead. No one was that gorgeous. That ripped. And he wasn't wearing much more than I was, his glorious muscles on display everywhere but the pair of tight shorts that barely reached the top of his thigh. And his---

O.M.G. That could *not* be real.

As I stared, it grew longer and wider as if reaching for me through the thin material.

Ummm, yeah. That was real. And I wanted it inside me now. Right freaking now.

He groaned. "What am I going to do with you, mate?"

"What?" Beyond bizarre. I did not respond to men like this. Especially not when I was bleeding, naked, in a strange place that looked like a—I took in what I could see of the small room—a tiny hospital room. My hand burned and itched like I'd dipped it in a barrel of hungry red ants. Rubbing my palm on the opposite elbow to preserve what little dignity I had left, I glared at my hallucination. He definitely had to be a figment of my imagination. Right? This all had to be some cruel joke God was playing on me because I'd stopped going to church when I was nineteen. No loving God I knew would leave so many kids in abusive homes or completely homeless, left to fend for themselves.

Basically, the almighty had pissed me off. Now the joke was on me.

Mister sex-on-a-stick moved forward, glanced at my bleeding ankle and shook his head.

"I'm dead, right? So, where am I? What is this place?" *And how did I rate such a sexy angel?*

Turning to me with a small device in his hand, he walked up to the coffin and reached to place the odd, magic wand looking thing next to my foot before turning it on. A blueish-green light blinked on around one end and he held it above the throbbing slices on my leg. Instantly the pain lessened, then faded completely. I sat up, arms still crossed over my breasts, and watched in fascination as the cuts magically closed. Within a few minutes the skin knit itself back together until it was smooth, as if nothing had been there at all.

Except the blood; it covered me from mid-calf down to my toes.

He turned to look at me and our faces were mere inches apart. "Are you hurt anywhere else?"

His gaze slammed into me and my nipples hardened to painful peaks. I pressed my thighs together as closely as I could to hide the wetness that gathered between my legs.

What was *wrong* with me?

He lifted a hand to cup my cheek, moving slowly like I was a skittish colt that might bolt at any moment. His thumb moved back and forth over my cheekbone in a caress that threatened to melt me into a puddle. "Answer me. Are you hurt anywhere else?"

I shook my head slightly, not enough to dislodge his hand, or the thumb now running back and forth over my lower lip.

Was he going to kiss me?

His lips looked soft and full and so close. His bare chest begging me to touch. To taste. I wanted to run my tongue across his chiseled muscles, see if he tasted as good as he smelled. All I had to do was lower my arms and *lean.*

Stop it! Had he drugged me or something?

"Who are you? And where am I?"

"Don't be afraid. You are safe now. You have been healing and resting in a ReGen pod. My name is Stark. The evil scum who tried to kill you will never get close to you again. I vow this to you mate, on my honor."

Mate? Honor? As to the two men who'd shot me, they weren't men at all. They were—

I leaned back, breaking contact. My lip tingled where he'd touched me. Ignoring the sensation, I looked around again. Odd designs were etched into walls that looked like they could be ceramic, or colored glass. The coffin I was still sitting in had strange figures on its side complete with bright, flashing lights and something that looked almost exactly like the readout on one of those hospital machines that beeped all the time and kept track of a patient's heartbeat.

I raised one hand to my neck and found my pulse. My frantic, threatening to jump out of my body, pulse. Once I found the bump and rhythm under my skin, I watched the blips on the screen.

Perfect match.

"Is this a hospital?"

"No."

"Where's Lilah?"

"Who?"

"My dog. Where is she? If you hurt her, I swear to God, I'll—"

Stark held his hands toward me, palms out. "Your pet is fine. She was shot and injured as well, but did not require the ReGen pod. Her injuries were not as severe as yours."

"I should be dead." That was a fact. I knew the moment I was shot that I was going to bleed out right there, my blood soaking into the dirt, the gravel digging into my face like tiny daggers.

"Indeed. I thank the gods you are not."

His lips were moving, but they didn't match what I was hearing. "Are you speaking English?"

"No. I am speaking Everian."

"Then how can I understand you?"

He lifted a hand and pointed to a spot just behind his ear. "Neural Processing Unit. The NPU links to the language centers in your brain, a kind of universal translator. I took the liberty of making sure you had one when I placed you in the healing pod."

I lifted my own hand, my fingertips locating the bump under my skin. Not there before. Definitely not. "That's what this thing is? A healing pod? Like in *Stargate*? When the bad Pharoah-bird guy lowers himself into the coffin and is totally healed?"

"I do not know to what you refer, but yes. The ReGen pod can heal most wounds."

I looked down at the pad I sat on with new respect and caught a glimpse of the partially shattered cover he had apparently tossed onto the floor when he opened it. I looked at the damage, then to him. "Sorry about that. I thought I was in a glass coffin. Buried alive, you know?"

"Rebecca, no. Who would do such a thing?"

I scoffed. How did he know my name? "You'd be surprised. Haven't you ever seen a vampire movie?" At his blank look I tried again. "How about a mafia movie?" I swung my legs over the side, careful to keep my feet together. I was naked. That was bad enough. He wasn't about to get a pussy peep show, too.

"No." His voice was gruff, lower. He stood as if frozen in place. Paralyzed.

My gaze landed on what was left of my clothing—it was in shreds with large burn marks and bloodstains all over it. Wouldn't be wearing that again. Next to the clothing was my purse, wallet on top and open. So that's how he knew who I was. I had to assume he also knew where I lived. My date of birth. Shit. My passport was in there, too. Although I wasn't sure why, since I never went anywhere. Somehow, carrying it around made the dream of traveling the world seem possible.

"May I please have some clothes?"

My request jolted him into action. "Of course." He left me alone for several minutes. When he returned he was completely dressed. Damn it. He carried an oversized black shirt draped over his shoulder, which he handed to me. "This is the only thing I have. My apologies. I did not expect to find you, and I have not installed an S-Gen machine capable of producing clothing on my ship."

I pulled the soft material on over my head and inhaled deeply. It smelled like him. Warm and spicy and irresistible. I wanted to bury my nose in it and just breathe. And I wanted him to take off his clothes again. I missed the view.

Once the shirt covered all the important parts, the hem of the much too large top resting in a pool around my hips, he held out his hand. "May I?"

Well, I sure didn't want to stay in the tiny coffin room. I placed my hand in his and stepped down, off the healing bed, onto the floor.

4

My bare feet had never felt anything so smooth and—

"It's warm."

"Yes, mate. I heated the floor for your comfort."

"You what?"

"If you prefer, I am happy to carry you again."

"Again?"

"When you were injured, I carried you here, to my ship." His hand settled at the curve of my back, low enough to make me want to press my body to his and see what happened. "You are very small. It is no burden to hold you in my arms."

Was that eagerness in his voice? Me? Small? Was he on drugs? I was well above average in every department. Height. Weight. Backside and cup size. Yet he towered over me, the top of my head not quite reaching his shoulder. I felt small. Feminine. I believed him when he said he could carry me.

Damn, that was *hot.*

"No, thank you. I can walk." Walk where, I had no idea. And why did he keep calling me his mate? I didn't volunteer for the Interstellar Brides Program. "Are you going to show me the rest of your spaceship?"

He led the way. I had seen the entire ship in a matter of minutes. A small cockpit with two seats and barely enough room to turn around. The medical bay we'd left, which was about the size of my mother's walk-in closet. He explained that the small S-Gen machine along the long stretch of hall would produce a variety of pre-programmed food. He then promised to get a larger ship with a proper S-Gen machine as soon as possible.

I had no idea what the hell he was talking about, so I nodded.

Two chairs and a tiny table could expand and retract into the wall in this same corridor. Out for eating, hidden away when not in use. His sleeping area held a long bed that would accommodate his height but was obviously designed for one person, not two.

Shut-up, horny. One look at his chest and all you can think about is riding his...

"Woof!" Lilah crawled out from under the bed and made her way to me.

"Lilah!" I rubbed her behind her ears, scratched her neck, reached around and hugged her, stroking her belly the way she liked.

She whimpered and I pulled back. "Oh no! I'm sorry baby. Are you hurt?"

Lilah pushed her nose into my palm for comfort and I looked her over. A large area on her side was bright pink skin with no hair. It looked fresh. And sore.

"What happened?"

"After you tried to kill yourself throwing your body in front of an ion blast, your pet attacked the male who injured you and was shot as well."

"What?" I looked down at my doe-eyed, two hundred pound baby. "You wouldn't hurt a fly, would you girl?"

Lilah wagged her tale and stared at me with all the love in her huge heart.

"She went for his throat, mate."

I sucked in a breath. Lilah? No way.

"She is very protective of you. I approve." He leaned in and patted Lilah on her neck. She allowed it, clearly familiar with his touch. I watched his large hand glide over her soft fur and clenched my teeth. This was the first time in my life I'd ever been jealous of a dog.

What else had happened while I was in that pod?

"Do not worry. I took his life. The other male escaped, but you were dying. I had to tend to you first. I carried you here and placed you in the ReGen pod. Lilah had to make due with the ReGen wand." He looked at Lilah, a sloppy grin on his face that I knew meant my girl had already worked her adorable magic on him. "Didn't you, big girl?"

Her tail wagged but I could tell she was tired. Using the familiar commands we had trained with, I whispered in her soft, floppy ear :"Go lay down, Lilah. Go to bed. I'll be back."

She turned around and shimmied her way back to

the space between the small bed and the floor, her new den. She had a kennel at home that she loved. It was her safe space, dark and cozy and private. I made a point not to bother her when she chose to go into her kennel. It was her way of saying she needed some quiet time, and I totally understood that.

Satisfied when I heard Lilah's soft snoring, we continued our tour.

"This is the containment area." He opened the door to a room with four cells, each barely large enough to hold one, maybe two people. If they were as big as he was? One. Definitely.

"Containment? Looks like a prison to me."

"I am an Elite Hunter. I track criminals and eliminate threats to the Coalition. My orders sometimes require bringing the subject back alive."

An Elite Hunter? Holy shit. When my friend Katie had volunteered, I'd read the brochures. I knew about the different alien types. "You're from Everis?" It finally registered that he had told me he was speaking Everian when I first came out of the pod. I guess my brain was still not fully awake, unlike my very turned-on body.

"Yes. You know of my planet?" He looked genuinely pleased, his smile making dangerous things inside me simmer. A vision of his bare chest flashed through my mind.

Again.

Like every five seconds.

"I've read about it." Why did I feel all warm and fuzzy inside just because I'd pleased him? I did my own thing, made my own way and paid my way through life. I did not bend over backwards to please a man, no matter how much I wanted to nibble on his chest.

Heaven help me, I was losing it.

He closed the door to the prison area and leaned into me until my back was pressed to the corridor's wall. "You know about Everis. Do you know about this?"

His fingers trailed softly from my upper arm, past my elbow, down to my wrist. He wrapped his fingers around my much smaller hand and lifted it so that my palm was held face up between us. My birthmark was there, an angry, irritated red from all the scratching and rubbing I'd subjected it to. Why hadn't that healing pod taken care of this, too?

"My birthmark?"

"Yes."

"What about it? I've had it forever."

Not letting go of my hand, he lifted his opposite hand into position mirroring mine. I gasped at the identical mark on his palm. "What? How is that possible?"

He leaned in closer, gently pressed his forehead to mine. Our breaths mingled. His heat, his scent, surrounded me. So hot. This was insane. I wanted him. I didn't know him. At all.

My body didn't care.

My birthmark throbbed, burned as if being so close to him was causing it to overheat. Those small bursts of fire traveled in a direct line to my core until I crossed my thighs and squeezed them together to try to find some relief. My breathing shaky, I stared in awe as the two birthmarks appeared to become darker and pulse in time with one another.

"What?" I lifted my face to his. Mistake. His lips were *right there.*

"These marks are sacred to all Everians. I do not know how it is possible, but you are mine and I am yours, Rebecca. We are marked mates. These marks prove it."

"Bullshit." I whispered the word but there was no venom in it. How could there be when I couldn't tear my gaze from his lips?

"I want to touch you." Stark moved so that his check pressed to mine, his voice a heated whisper against my ear. "I want to taste you." His hand moved to the outer edge of my thigh and moved slowly up, lifting the shirt with it.

My entire being shuddered with pure, raw lust. A momentary flash of sanity reminded me how thankful I was for my IUD. I could take what I wanted from him without worrying about—

"I want to fuck you, Rebecca. Bury my cock deep. Swallow your cries of pleasure with my kiss." Stark's hot palm slipped beneath the shirt to stroke the curve of my ass. My knees nearly gave out.

"I will make you come over and over. I will fuck you and I will not stop until you beg."

As if the word was some kind of signal, Stark stopped moving. He froze in place like a warm blanket, taunting me with his masculine scent and the hot touch of his palm on my ass.

He was waiting for me to decide. Yes or no. Take what he was offering or shy away from such intimacy until another time. Another day.

Who was I kidding? Another *life*.

I'd never felt like this. Not with the awkward boyfriends I'd had in high school. Not with the slightly less awkward men I'd dated since. And the smooth-talking players? Forget it. I could see those fools coming from a mile away. One night stands were not my style. Or at least they hadn't been. But that was before I'd thought I was going to die, before I'd been shot by aliens, before I'd met *him*.

I didn't make a habit of lying to myself and I wasn't about to start now. I wanted him. I wanted *all* that. The kissing and the fucking and the begging. I wanted to touch him everywhere. Taste his skin. Let him do pretty much whatever he wanted to me because that purr in his voice promised he'd be good. *Really good.* And I believed him.

"Rebecca?" My name was a husky whisper against my ear.

"Yes. To all of it." I turned my head to claim his lips in a kiss as a shudder passed through him. That was my shudder. I'd done that to the sexiest man I'd ever laid eyes on. *Me.*

Mouths locked together, I felt as if we were in a race with no finish line. The only thing I wanted to do was keep going. Our tongues dueled and wrapped around one another. He lifted me, carrying me down the small corridor as I wrapped my legs around his hips. His cock rubbed along the wet heat of me as he walked, a sweet torture that made me groan.

True to his word, he swallowed down the sound with his kisses.

He stopped outside the door to his sleeping room but

I shook my head. "No. Lilah's in there. She'll watch. Or want to wedge her body between us."

He chuckled but walked to the eating area and pressed the controls that brought the small table out of its hiding place in the wall.

"What are you doing?" The pseudo-kitchen table? Really?

He laid me down on my back, shoved the shirt I wore up to my neck and then dropped to his knees between my legs. He lifted my thighs over his shoulders. His dark gaze burned into mine. "I'm hungry."

Stark lowered his head, gaze holding mine as he locked his lips over my core. Plunged his tongue deep. Sucked my clit into his mouth. Played with it, with me. Two fingers slid deep as he worked me with his mouth.

I reached for him, for his shoulder. His hair. Anything I could grab hold of to anchor myself to reality. Our palms touched.

Something burned. Flared. Was I dying? Losing my mind? Nothing could feel like this.

I stopped breathing, the air locked in my throat as the taste of my pussy exploded inside my mind. I shared his primitive need to taste me, to hear me cry out in pleasure. I felt the actual pain of those needs. In his heart. His chest. His cock. His focus was absolute. Complete. There was nothing in his world but me. My body. My pleasure.

Mate.

Never had I been as beautiful, as perfect, as I appeared to him. My dark skin glowed with health, the softness seductive. My heavy breasts called to him to suckle, tease, conquer. The taste of my kiss mingled with my core in the perfect love potion. He was addicted. Couldn't get enough. Would *never* get enough.

The overload of sensation—his and mine—pushed me into orgasm. His tongue worked my clit as my inner muscles spasmed. There was no relief, no cool down. He pushed me over again. My back arched up off the table. A shocked cry left my throat.

He stood, pulled his cock free from his black pants. I had barely registered that fact before I was reaching for him. Begging him to fill me up. Take me. Make me his.

Feet digging into his hips, I tried to make him move faster. Deeper. Harder.

He refused, the blunt tip of him barely there. Inside me but not *inside* me.

"Stark." His name was a whimper.

Suddenly he was there, in my mind the way I'd been in his, as he thrust deep, filled me up to the edge of pain. He was huge. Hard. So good. God, so good.

"Give me your hand." It was nothing less than a command. I didn't even think to deny him. He pressed the back of my hand to the table and covered my palm with his. Our marks touched. Flared. Heated once more. His fingers tangled with mine and we both held on as he moved faster and faster, pumping into me like a machine.

My orgasm roared through me out of nowhere. No warning. No build-up. Just there, making me shatter in his arms, break into a thousand tiny pieces, our locked hands the only thing holding me together.

He followed me this time, his cock jumping inside my swollen core, filling me with his seed. And then it was over.

Cock still inside me, he leaned over and took my lips in a series of kisses so soft, so reverent, tears gathered in my eyes. A strong rhythmic pulse flowed through our birthmarks, gently now, quiet as if they, too, were temporarily sated.

A heavy ache settled in the center of my chest, a wound, long ignored, now ripped open and bleeding. Bare. Exposed.

The way Stark touched me, the way he kissed me, the way his hands moved over my body—as if I was precious and perfect? It hurt. Hurt like hell because I realized no one had ever really loved me before. Not like this. Marked Mates. Rare. Destined to be together. Perfect for one another.

I'd thought he was spouting nonsense. I'd been wrong. So freaking wrong.

Worse, he was an alien. I had a dog and a new house waiting for me. A new life. New town. College classes. A future I'd fought hard for.

How was it possible that in just a few hours and I didn't *want* to stay here, move, go to classes, exist... without *him*. Insane. This was completely crazy. I didn't even *know him*.

A loud, desolate howl filled the ship. *Lilah*.

She howled again, made it sound like she was dying of loneliness. She knew I couldn't resist that forlorn, desperate sound.

That dog was too smart for her own good.

Her third howl would have made an unsuspecting human worry that she was being tortured. I burst out laughing, the movement reminding me of exactly what

Stark and I had been doing, and that he was still deep inside me.

His gaze locked on mine and he grinned. "I suppose you love that creature and will not entertain the idea of giving your pet to another?"

"Yes. I do love her. And no, I'm never giving her up."

Suddenly serious, he leaned close and kissed me one more time. "How did she manage that?"

"She loved me first. Dogs aren't like people. They don't lie or hold grudges. They just love you."

He pressed his cheek to mine, his lips brushing my ear, his cock still buried deep as if he never wanted to leave. "I can love you like that. If you'll let me."

I didn't know what to think or say. I was in over my head. Way over my freaking head.

He stepped back, separating us and I held back a groan. I didn't want this to be over. Not yet.

A gentle hand lifted my ankle and he frowned. "I should have taken care of you first."

"What?"

"The blood, mate. I do not like the sight of it on your perfect skin."

Before I could protest he disappeared. He came back a few moments later with a warm cloth and held my ankle as he wiped away the dried blood with soft strokes. He produced a second and stroked his seed from my thighs. I was grateful for his thoughtfulness. I didn't have clothes here and I had no idea where the bathroom was.

Wait.

"Where is the bathroom?"

"If you would like to cleanse yourself, I have a cleansing pod."

"Pods. What is it with all the pods?"

"There is not a lot of room on a spaceship." His dark eyes were full of humor and suddenly I desperately wanted to see him laughing. Head thrown back, from the belly, pure joyous laughter.

I really didn't want to have to state the obvious, but there was no help for it. "No, I mean, where is the toilet?"

"One is not required. We eliminated the need for such a mess centuries ago."

"What?"

His smile was pure sin as one hand slid up my thigh. "If you need release, mate, I am happy to provide."

Oh my god, he was terrible. And I loved it. "I usually go to the toilet after...you know."

He grew serious. "Do you feel the need? That should not be happening." He helped me from the table and wrapped me in his arms. I settled against his chest like he'd hugged me this way a thousand times. "I will take you back to my medical station and run scans at once."

"What?" Confused, I held myself still for a moment and took stock of my body. I didn't feel...anything.

"Coalition transport technology automatically empties and recycles all of our biological waste. I programmed the ReGen pod to make sure you had the proper micro-implants for space travel."

"What?"

"If you feel the need to empty your body of waste, the implants are not working properly."

"What!" My confused voice was half-muddled by his hard, hot, wide chest.

Stark loosened his hold and placed his hands on each of my shoulders so he could look directly into my eyes. "You say that word a lot, mate. I'm not sure you know what it means."

I placed a hand flat on his chest, ground my teeth to prevent myself from stroking him, and spoke through my clenched jaw. "Stark?"

"Yes, love?"

Deep breathe. This was insane. All of it. "Are you telling me I have some kind of microscopic alien technology inside my body that magically zaps all of my body's natural waste and sends it to some kind of alien recycling plant?" That just sounded...*gross*. Who wanted recycled poo?

Then again, as a woman who needed to empty my bladder far too many times a day, the idea of not having to pee was a bit *too* appealing.

"Exactly. Are you hungry?"

"You can't magically zap food into my stomach?"

He smiled. "The technology is available, but most prefer to indulge in tasting their food and drink."

"That was supposed to be a joke."

"As that was not amusing in the slightest, I must assume my NPU is malfunctioning and I do not understand the use of that word."

My jaw dropped. "Are you for real right now?" *Alien. Alien. Alien.* How could he be so sexy and irresistible and so...weird?

Right. He was a freaking alien.

In response to my question, he took one of my hands and held my palm over the place I assumed his heart would be. If he was human. Or human-ish? "I am very real. And I am yours."

The moment I touched him our gazes locked. My mind went blank. All I wanted to do was melt into him again. Kiss him. Touch him. Beg him to put me back on that table, spread my legs wide open and—

A forlorn howl filled the ship, breaking the spell.

"You are lethal," I whispered. Absolute truth.

"Very. I hunt. Sometimes, to protect our people, I am forced to kill." His gaze darkened and I felt something like fear flash through our strange bond. He squeezed my hand, pressed it more firmly to his chest. "To protect you, mate, I would destroy worlds."

What the actual hell was I supposed to say to *that?* My usual go-to in tense situations was to crack a joke. But when an alien was threatening to blow up planets, being a wise-ass didn't feel appropriate. He was serious. His sincerity throbbed in my blood in time to the pulsing of the marks on our palms.

"How about you finish the hunt for your bad guys and leave the destruction of planets for another day?" I lifted my free hand to the base of his neck and ran my fingers through his dark hair. My touch seemed to help. He lowered his head until our foreheads touched, a pose I was rapidly becoming addicted to.

"First I must take care of you. Are you hungry?"

Another long howl filled the air.

I smiled. "A little. But I think Lilah is. I fed her this morning but she doesn't like to skip meals. And I don't know the last time she was outside." I walked the short distance to Stark's bedroom and opened the door. Lilah bounded out and into my legs like a tank, nearly tipping me over. Big lug. I bent down and wrapped my arms around her in a calming hug. First she needed to take a trip outside to relieve herself. Unless she had the weird recycling going on, too? But food. My poor baby needed food and water and she did *not* like to skip meals.

"Your pet has been taken care of. I give you my word."

I smiled a thank you at my big space boyfriend and stood. A step and a half and I had my hand on the panel next to what he'd told me was basically the front door of his ship.

"No!"

Stark reached for me but it was too late. The door slid open and I stood, uncomprehending.

Blackness.

Pinpoints of light.

And...nothing.

No. This couldn't be. It had to be my imagination. I was in a dream. That's what this was. A dream.

Lilah came to me and sat at my side, as she'd done thousands of times. She whimpered, her huge head nudging me for attention. That felt real. Too real.

No, no, no, no, no.

5

I SHOULD HAVE TOLD her the moment she woke. But she'd already been panicked, breaking the ReGen pod and injuring her leg.

I'd touched her then. Gods help me, I hadn't been able to resist taking her. Claiming her. Making sure she could never escape our bond, even after she discovered the truth. I was an Elite Hunter. I had a duty to my people and several more years on my enlistment. I had a duty to the Coalition, to the billions we protected on hundreds of member planets. I could not remain on Earth with her. And I could not live without her. Be alone. Not now that I knew she existed.

She would need to leave her home, her world and everyone she loved to be with me. I'd been a coward, terrified of her choice.

"Are we...are we in space?" Rebecca turned to me, her dark eyes wide with shock. Lilah nudged her, offering comfort. My mate did not respond to her beloved pet. That alone told me I'd made a mistake.

A huge fucking mistake.

"Rebecca, let me explain."

"You took me into outer space?" She clenched her hands into fists at her sides as she stared out at a sight all to familiar to me. Blackest night sprinkled with stars. Planets that twinkled light years away. Emptiness. Loneliness. Cold, black nothing.

"You carried me to your little spaceship, stuck me in that pod and took me into outer freaking space?" Her voice grew louder and higher pitched with each word.

"The criminals from Siren legion remain on Earth. I could not protect you and hunt them at the same time. I am taking you home. Once you are safe, I will resume my hunt."

"What?"

"There is that word again." I truly must check in with the NPU techs once back on Everis.

"Taking me home?" She pointed outside the ship to what lay beyond the energy shield protecting us. "Does that look like *home* to you?"

It did. I'd spent years out here hunting. Tracking. Killing. I'd never truly felt alone until I met her. Now that emptiness made a mockery of the expanse outside this ship. Inside me, a yawning pit grew in my gut, twisting and pinching my insides until I fought to breathe.

I stared at her long legs, the tops of her thighs barely covered by my shirt. I loved seeing her wearing nothing else, covered in my scent, her hair in total disarray from the wildness of her passion. Her breasts were full and round and tempted me to lift the garment, kneel before her and take them into my mouth. To rouse her passion so that this conversation could be forgotten and begun anew.

"Well?" She put her hands on her hips, an oddly adorable huff passing her lips. "What were you thinking?"

I had only one answer. "*You* are my home now. I cannot lose you, and I could not protect you on Earth, not the way I should."

"So where are you taking me?"

"Home, to Everis."

"Mmm-hmm." She stared out into deep space for another few moments before lifting her hand to the sensor and closing the door. "You, Elite Hunter Stark, are going to take me home. To Earth. To my house. Right now."

"I explained this to you. I cannot protect you there."

She turned to face me, hands still on her hips. She tilted her head to the side and glared at me through a fall of dark curls. "And I can't protect my kids from up here."

"Kids? You have children? A mate?" A dagger-like pain stabbed through my chest but I kept my face calm, expressionless.

"Oh, no." She shook her head and my heart began to beat again. "I take care of the neighborhood kids down at the youth center. Well, I did. Yesterday was my last day."

"Yesterday?"

"Yes. Before the whole aliens almost killing me incident?"

Dread chilled my blood to a sluggish crawl in my veins. I stepped close enough to reach her but did not pull her into my arms as I wished. "Mate, your injuries were extensive. You were in the ReGen pod for more than one day."

"How long?" She wrapped her arms around herself as if she needed someone to hold her. I reached out but she stepped out of reach and Lilah growled a warning.

Protective beast. I no longer approved of her behavior. My mate's pet would need to be taught that I was never a threat—

"Stark. How. Long?"

I stopped glaring at her pet and looked my mate in the eyes. She deserved the truth. "Five days have passed on Earth since you were injured." Five days of hell as I waited, worried that my mate would die, would disappear from my life before I'd had a chance to know her. I could not hunt and leave her unprotected on my ship. An even greater weakness I now must confront? I did not wish to leave her side, not even to hunt.

"Five days?" Rebecca twisted her hands in front of her and muttered to herself as she paced back and forth in the small corridor. "This can't be right. Five days? Shit. I need to call the cops." She stopped pacing and looked up at me. "Do you have a phone on this thing?"

"If you are referring to a communication device capable of contacting humans through your primitive technology, then yes. However, I was not on Earth to speak to humans. I was sent to hunt."

"Well, I need to call the cops and turn those guys in. They are still out there selling that awful drug to my kids." She looked around the corridor as if something new might appear in the barren space. "Where's my purse? I need my cell phone." She looked up at me. "Can I use my cell phone? Will it work with your ship's...whatever?"

"No. And I cannot allow you to involve the humans. They are no match for what they will face. Every human you send after those responsible will die."

"Five days." She lifted her hands to cover her face. "Oh, god. The movers. I was supposed to meet them."

"Movers?"

"All my stuff. The landlord told me he had new tenants all lined up. Shit. What if they just took all my stuff? Where would they take it? Some auction place?"

"We will take it back." No one was going to steal anything from my mate.

"The safe! Stark. Shit. The safe! It has that alien thing in it."

"What thing?" Every instinct I had went on high alert.

"I don't know. Andreas said he stole it from them. I didn't know what to do with it so I locked it up at the center." She passed by me again, increased the pace of her steps. This time I grabbed her upper arm when she made the turn and pulled her close.

"Rebecca?"

"What are we going to do if they go to center to get it back? What if they break in? Or hurt the kids? I don't even know what it is. I don't think Andreas did either. He's a curious kid. That's probably why he stole it."

"What did he steal?" My shoulders stiffened and I made an effort to keep my voice soft. "Tell me what he took from them."

"We need to go talk to him. He should be home. I got a text. They were sending him home that night. He should still be there, right? He wouldn't be dumb enough to try to go back, would he? Or take any more of that stupid Quell?"

"Rebecca!" I used my command voice and my mate jumped.

"What?"

"Look at me."

Slowly, she lifted her face, our gazes locked. "We have to go back. Now. Right now."

Her dark brown eyes were deep enough to drown in. Her soft body pressed to mine and my cock grew hard once more. I wanted her again. I would always want her. Would never get enough of her taste, her scent, her voice. She was courageous and loyal as well, throwing her body in front of the ion blast meant for her pet. Protecting 'her kids' with a savageness only mothers possess.

What would she be willing to sacrifice to protect a mate she loved? Or our children?

I knew the answer. Everything. Which meant I could never leave her alone again. She would not hesitate to step in harm's way, or to risk her life to protect someone she cared about. That was not acceptable.

"Describe the item in your safe to me."

"I don't know. It's a weird shape, like in that *Superman* movie where he finds his father's ship and puts the long thing into the thing and it activates the hologram." She ranted and tried to pull away in the direction of the piloting controls.

"What language are you speaking?" She made no sense. Perhaps I needed to run a complete update on my NPU.

"English." She stepped back. This time I let her go. She returned to pacing, her path shorter, her hands moving through her hair over and over as if she were trying to comfort herself.

Watching her move was hypnotic. Seductive. Focusing on the conversation was an effort. She had bewitched me. How was I going to hunt when the only thinking organ in my body was my cock?

"I need to get dressed. I can't go home like this." Her pet moved at last, the lazy beast stepping between me and my female in an obvious warning. She rubbed Lilah on her giant head and they both disappeared inside my small bedchamber. I heard slamming as my mate opened and closed the mostly empty storage compartments. "Don't you have any clothes on this ship?" she yelled.

I leaned against the doorframe and watched her stretch to reach the higher compartments. Nice view. Very nice. "None that would fit you."

"Stark! Stop staring at my boobs, this is serious."

"No. And yes."

"What?"

"No, I very much enjoy looking at you mate. I will not stop. And yes, this is serious. Yet you have told me nothing that makes sense."

She threw her hands over her head and made a loud

groaning sound. "Men! I swear to god, you are all the same. Doesn't matter what planet you are from."

Calling upon my Elite Hunter speed, I moved past her pet and had her in my arms before she finished speaking. The squeak that came from her throat pushed my predator's instincts to the limit. I'd caught her. Time to claim my reward.

Burying one fist in her hair, I tilted her head and claimed her mouth. Shoved my tongue deep, mimicked what I wanted to do to her body with my cock. She stiffened in my arms, a deep cry coming from her throat. The sound immediately melted into a whimper and she melted into me, locked her arms around me and kissed me back.

Bad idea, Stark.

My body disagreed.

It had already been five days. What was a few more minutes when my cock throbbed, my heart ached and I could not think when she kissed me like *this*.

Demanding. Eager. Desperate.

Maybe that was me.

Breaking the kiss, I lifted her so that she was on her hands and knees on top of my bed, her hair a cascade down her back, her round ass on perfect display. And the glistening, pink center of her broke my will.

I filled her in one deep stroke. Her soft cry urged me on. Faster. Harder. I wanted to be so deeply a part of her that she would never doubt, never fear losing me, never want another.

"Stark, we can't..."

"We can." I had no choice. I pushed my shirt high on

her shoulders so I could stroke her skin. She had awakened a part of me that did not listen to reason. The Hunter. The wild thing inside me normally came alive only to track. Pursue. Find people who did not wish to be found and bring them to justice.

This...I ran my palms over my mate's soft back. Her bottom. Her thighs. *This* was better.

"But—"

"I need you, mate. I need you like this."

She gave in to the pleasure I offered, dropping her chest low. She rested on bent elbows as I pumped into her body like an animal. I wouldn't last long, she was too hot. Too wet. Her scent was making my head explode with primitive images of all the ways I would take her, now that she was mine.

She slid her arm out from under her torso, moved her hand lower to stroke the sensitive nub between her legs.

The sight of her giving herself pleasure drove me to madness. My mate. *Mine.*

I held on until she cried out, until the swollen walls of her core pulsed and spasmed around my hard length. Grabbing her hips, I lifted her off the bed and pulled her ass tightly to me. Buried deep, I came, my shout a shock of sound I'd never made before.

When it was over, I leaned down to rest my forehead against her curved back. Gods, she was beautiful.

"You are dangerous, female."

She chuckled and the movement in her core made me groan. "I didn't start that."

"You did."

"How?"

"By being too beautiful to resist."

The compliment appeared to leave her speechless. I placed a soft kiss on her dark skin. Drawn to her like a magnet, I lingered. Breathed her in. Moved a bit. Kissed her again.

"If you don't stop, we will never get out of this room." Her voice was soft and accepting. Sexy. I could listen to her sound like that for the rest of my life.

"You would tempt me with paradise?"

A distinctly non-human whimper filled the small space. I looked over to see her giant pet staring at us, her dark eyes assessing me with a look I had never seen before.

Was that animal *glaring* at me.

"Oh my god! I forgot she was in here!" Rebecca groaned. "Look at her. She knows. She knows what we were doing! Get off of me. This is embarrassing."

"Your pet will get used to seeing us thus." Reluctant to leave the warmth of her body, I pulled my cock free and looked at the animal whose head was perched at an odd angle, titled to one side as she stared at us with those huge, brown eyes, unblinking.

"And we were doing it *doggie-style!* Oh, god. That's even worse."

"What are you upset about?" I truly did not understand her reference. "What is '*doing it*'? Are you referring to our mating? And what is '*doggie-style*'?"

She burst out laughing. My mate rolled over onto her side and propped herself up on one arm to look at me. Her dark hair framed her face perfectly. "What am I supposed to do with you, huh?"

Fully clothed once more, I sat next to her on the small bed and gently pushed a stray piece of hair from her face. "Keep me. Allow me to stay at your side."

Rebecca flopped onto her back and stared up at me, her heart in her eyes. "No wonder I can't seem to stay mad at you."

Did she know what her gaze told me? Was she beginning to love me? Did I dare hope? I could not lose that fragile beginning within her. I needed her too badly. "We will return to Earth."

She gasped and reached for me, her palm tender against my cheek. "Thank you."

I sighed. When she looked at me like that I could deny her nothing. Already I was hers in ways she could not comprehend. The pull of a Marked Mate was no small thing. A miracle. Rare. True and strong and impossible to deny. I would give her anything. Follow her anywhere. Kill for her. Die for her. Never get enough of her voice. Her touch. Her scent. Her smile.

I wanted more. I wanted her heart.

"We return. Not for the hunt. Not for the Coalition. We go back because I know your heart would break if we did not."

Tears gathered in her eyes and I cursed myself a fool. What the fuck had I done wrong now? I had killed the one who attacked her. Saved her life and that of her beloved animal. I had healed them both. Cared for them. Stated my intention and claimed her body, giving her pleasure. I had melded our hearts into one with the binding of our marks as I filled her with my cock. What more could I have done in such a short time?

Nothing. I had done all I could do. It was not enough.

Despair threatened to break me at the great sorrow I saw gathering in her eyes.

A single tear slid down her cheek. Two. I could not bear it. "Please, do not." I wiped the tears away with my thumb. "Do not cry. I will fix this. Whatever is breaking your heart, I will fix it."

She smiled. "I don't think so, Stark." She turned her head and placed a kiss in the palm of my hand, my skin wet with the tears I'd wiped away. "I think this might be what love feels like. I just didn't expect it to hurt."

"I do not know. I have never been in love before." Before her.

She sniffled and wiped the remainder of her tears away. She sat up, a new energy singing in every line of her body. She pulled my shirt down to cover herself and slapped the bed. "Okay. You, go set the autopilot, or whatever you guys call it, to take us back to Earth."

"The journey will take five days." I did not want to disappoint her with the news, but she needed to know. "We are nearly home."

"To Everis?"

"Yes."

"Okay. It is what it is. Get us turned around and then come find me."

"The ship is not large enough for you to hide from me."

"I know. I'll even tell you where to look."

Confused, I felt my own head tilt to the side, just as her pet's did. "Where?"

"In the shower. Thanks to you, I need one. Badly."

The assault on my senses began at once as I imagined water gliding over her curves. Droplets on her lips. Moving my hands over every part of her. Relishing the soft glide of cleansing oils on her smooth skin.

My cock pulsed. I swore at the shameless beast. The vision would not leave me. The curse of a vivid imagination.

"Perhaps that is not a good idea." I turned my face away. The only way to regain control of myself was to stop looking. I could not think with her spread out on my bed like an offering to a god. To me.

"I don't know. I'd like to try out those oils."

"What?" My head snapped to attention. I turned to look at her over my shoulder. She was grinning, a sexy, feminine grin full of pure seduction.

"I don't know what you did to us when you put our birthmarks together, but I can't seem to get you completely out of my head. And sometimes, I see things." She shrugged. "I assume they are coming from you. Some kind of alien sex side effect. If not, I've got a serious problem on my hands."

6

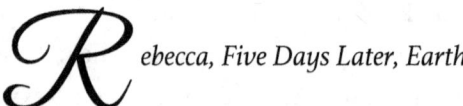

THE SPACESHIP SETTLED in an empty section of a large open area inside the Interstellar Bride's Processing center's compound. He turned on the monitors so I could see the small army of giants moving to surround us.

Us. *Our* ship. When had that happened?

Sure, it was small, but it felt like home now. Even Lilah had settled in. I didn't mind the small bed because Stark held me all night long. When I complained of being too hot, he made sure the room was cool enough for my comfort. He looked after me constantly, asking if I was hungry or thirsty or tired. Making love to me multiple times a day. Even using that funny magic wand to heal my lady parts when they got sore from all the unusual activity.

Hah. I smiled. The last 10 days had been filled with pounding and grinding and so many orgasms I'd literally lost count. Which was completely crazy when I realized I could count on one hand the number of orgasms I'd had in bed with a man in the last five *years*.

"Are you sure about this?" Stark asked.

"Yes. Trust me. She is famous. Seems like a really cool chick."

"She is a child from one of the bird races?"

"No. What? There are bird people?"

"Of course."

"Why aren't they in the brochures?" Bird people? Holy shit. What else was out there?

"They are not part of the Coalition of Planets. Their home worlds are in a distant galaxy and they had no desire to become involved in our war with the Hive."

Bird people. Wow.

I moved to stand next to the pilot's seat and rested one hand on his shoulder, the hand with the birthmark, the one that had made Stark mine. I'd hated the odd mark my entire life. Now I was grateful to have it. Happy.

Stark lifted one hand to cover mine, his touch both familiar and comforting. "How many Prillon and Atlan guards does one woman need?"

I looked at the monitors again and had to agree. Walking toward us, head held high, was the woman I recognized from the brochures my friend Katie had shown me before she volunteered to be a bride. The woman was Warden Egara, a human in charge of processing all the volunteer brides in North America. She was based in Miami, which wasn't exactly Cleveland. I was still far from home, but Stark had a plan and I had convinced him these people—or aliens—would help.

Stark settled the ship and went outside to speak to her. I stayed in the cockpit, as agreed, not because I was afraid to go outside, but because I still didn't have anything to wear and I was not flashing my ass to every alien in the joint.

Stark spoke briefly to Warden Egara. I watched her pass a bag to him. He was back in minutes. Eagerly, I pulled the ordered clothing from the bag and put everything on. It all fit perfectly, even the bra and panties.

"I like you better naked, mate."

I smiled at my man. My alien man. "Don't worry, as soon as we're alone again I'll switch back to my normal clothing."

"You mean one of my shirts with nothing beneath?"

"Of course."

His smile made my heart melt a little more than it should. I was already in love with him. I knew it. But every time I thought I was in as deep as I could go, he did or said something that made me want him more. I hadn't thought about college or the cheap items I'd packed up to move since the day I woke in the glass coffin. There was one box of personal items I cared about, photos and little things I'd managed to keep after my parents died. I did want that. The rest? Nothing but random stuff of my random life before *him*.

Hopefully Warden Egara had sent the message ahead to Cleveland for me and one of my friends from the center had been able to pick it up. Wherever it was.

I smoothed the ivory blouse and rust colored pants over my curves and felt normal again. Well, as normal as I could with an alien staring at me and Lilah flopped down in the corridor of a spaceship like a huge dog carpet.

I slipped my feet into an extremely comfortable pair of sandals and smiled up at Stark. "These are perfect."

"Of course. I was very specific when I sent your measurements."

"But you didn't measure me."

He smiled and pulled me in for a kiss. "Of course I did, mate. Every single part of you is branded inside me."

See? How the hell was I supposed to resist a guy who said that kind of ridiculous thing and actually *meant it.*

He got a kiss for his trouble.

"Okay. Let's go talk to her." I placed my hand in Stark's and allowed him to lead me to the exit. "What did she say? Were they able to find it?"

"No."

"No? I told them exactly where it was."

"Apparently, when the safe was opened, it was empty."

"What?"

He chuckled. "If you continue to use that word so frequently I shall start charging a fee."

"Like a cuss jar?"

"I do not know of what you speak."

"Never mind." We were walking down the ramp of a spaceship just like in a movie. There was practically an army of gigantic, armed aliens waiting for us, and one small woman. Pretty. Dark hair. Gray eyes. Maybe a year or two older than me. I was nervous and needed a distraction. "What's the fee?"

He didn't hesitate. Apparently he'd been thinking about this for a while. "A kiss."

I chuckled. "Why would you ask for that when you can already have as many as you want."

He stopped dead in his tracks at the bottom of the ramp and turned me to face him. "Can I?"

I saw something in his eyes I hadn't seen before, vulnerability. "Yes."

"And tomorrow? Once your drug dealers are dead?"

My heart sank. I wanted to be with him, but moving to outer space? God, moving across the country had seemed nearly impossible a few days ago. Another planet was next level scary.

"Excuse me for interrupting but we don't have a lot of time." We both turned to find Warden Egara had approached, two massive Prillon guards on either side of her. Four guards? Just for Stark?

I held out my hand. "Hi. I'm Rebecca. This is Stark."

The warden accepted my proffered hand and shook it briefly before turning to Stark. "Elite Hunter Stark. Welcome. I have been in contact with Prillon Prime and confirmed your assignment."

Next to me, Stark stiffened. "I do not lie, warden."

She watched Stark with narrowed eyes, completely unphased by his stern tone. "We have had a large amount of unexpected activity here on Earth the last few months, including dealings with the legions on Rogue 5. Forgive me for being thorough."

When Stark stared back, I stepped between them and smiled. "It's okay. Don't mind him. He's just trying to protect me and kill the jerks selling Quell."

Warden Egara's gray eyes locked on me. "Of course. And you are his marked mate?"

I held up my hand, palm out to show her my birthmark as Stark wrapped an arm around me and pulled me to his side.

"She is mine."

Warden Egara laughed, her entire demeanor completely changed from stern to gorgeous. "I can see that. Excellent." She looked at me with a much softer, much kinder smile. "I am very protective of my brides, Rebecca. I had to make sure you were all right."

"I'm not an Interstellar Bride."

"Are you not?" She looked from me to Stark and raised her eyebrows. I didn't feel like arguing.

"I'm fine. Stark has taken very good care of me."

From behind, Lilah nudged my thigh with her head before moving to place herself between me and the nearest pair of Prillon guards. I had to admit, they were intimidating. Even taller than Stark with sharp features and oddly colored skin. Some of them looked almost human with dark brown skin, or light beige that could have been fair skin with a good tan. But the others? Copper. Golden. Strange colored eyes to match. And the Atlans behind them? Well, they looked more human, but they had to be seven feet tall. At least. A couple of them looked closer to eight.

And they transformed into something even *bigger*?

Lord help the girl who got herself mated to one of them. Then again, that's why they were called beasts.

"And is this the big girl who got herself shot by those terrible, mean aliens?" Warden Egara had her hands all over Lilah, scratching her behind the ears—and Lilah was eating it up.

Traitor.

Some attack dog.

Warden Egara—still bent over to pet my traitorous dog—grinned up at me. Let's go inside. It's too hot out here." She glanced at Stark. "We have taken your concerns into account, Elite Hunter. We have more than enough manpower here to help you catch your criminals and protect your mate."

I looked around at the aliens standing guard out here under the bright sunshine. There had to be even more alien warrior guys inside. It was a large facility. I glanced up at Stark to find his lips not quite as thin and his shoulders more relaxed. He really had been worried about protecting me while he hunted.

He was adorable. In a totally scary way that made me want to rip his clothes off and make him chase me. Stark had warned me never to run from him unless I wanted to be caught and fucked into extreme bliss. Running would activate his Elite Hunter instincts. I'd seen him move too fast to track with the naked eye. I didn't know what else he could do, but these aliens all seemed to show Stark a high level of respect. And Stark? No fear. None. Which was saying something, because these aliens were huge, scary and built like tanks.

Every single one of them made sure to keep a significant distance from my man.

Ouch. Stark was hot. Lethal. And *mine*.

We followed Warden Egara inside and I ignored the fact that my brand new panties were already more than a little wet.

7

My small ship had never carried this many. Warden Egara had offered to keep Rebecca safe in Miami. My stubborn mate, however, had adamantly refused to be left behind.

So here we were, crammed inside my ship with six Atlan Warlords, each one competing for Lilah's attention. They were going to fatten our pet twice her already monstrous size if they didn't stop using my S-Gen machine to make her favorite dog treats. Rebecca had taught them all of her pet's commands and they were jostling one another aside like children to watch the drooling creature sit. Stand. Lay down. Back up. Roll over.

Play dead. That one was their favorite. I had to admit, the sight of Lilah lying on her back with her tongue hanging limply from the side of her mouth was highly amusing.

And Rebecca? She watched their foolish antics and laughed. Eyes sparkling, head thrown back. She was smore beautiful than ever and I could not bring myself to ruin her fun.

The Atlans? I would have tossed them in the containment cells in the back if Rebecca would allow it. I'd seen more than one admiring my mate. She was stunning. I couldn't blame them for their appreciation, but I didn't have to like it.

"We're nearly there. Get on mission."

Lilah, *dead* on the floor, twisted her body just enough to look at me upside-down. Rebecca sat back down in the co-pilot's seat and buckled in, the smile on her face mellowing to a grin. Then worry.

The Atlans responded to their training, accepting the command and leaving Lilah alone to check their weapons and armor one more time.

Apparently nervous, Rebecca bit her bottom lip and leaned closer to the vid screens as the youth center came into view. "It looks so small from up here."

"We will be there in just a couple of minutes. Review for us, one more time, the exact location of the safe."

Rebecca recited the same information to all of us as she'd done at least a dozen times when we'd still been in Florida with the warden. "As long as it's after ten, there shouldn't be anyone there."

I scanned the human communication frequencies and located the local time. "It is eleven fourteen."

"Good." Rebecca visibly relaxed, leaning back in her seat. "What does the AI thing do again?"

Velik's tone was kind when he answered my mate. Which was good, otherwise I would have to break his knees so he could kneel before her and beg forgiveness. "The engram holds the core components for their ship's artificial intelligence system. The AI runs the ship, makes all the calculations required for space travel and controls the ship's systems. Without it, their craft won't operate."

"And that AI is actually smart enough to know it's trapped in my safe and send out a distress signal?"

"Indeed."

"That is *Terminator* level scary." She glanced back at one of the Atlans who had insisted on carrying an extremely large ion rifle. The biggest one I'd ever seen.

He grinned. "We are the only terminators here, my lady."

I shook my head.

Rebecca chuckled. "*Terminator* is a movie about a robot that travels back in time to kill the leader of a human revolution."

The Atlan shifted his rifle to his opposite side. "I do not travel through time, but I am very skilled at killing."

Rebecca paused, stared at the huge grin on the Atlan's face. "Good to know."

No doubt she believed the Atlan jested. I knew the opposite to be true. And if the Siren scum were here to retrieve the AI engram for their ship—a fact we'd figured out in Florida as well—we might need that ridiculous rifle. And all six Atlans.

Fuck. Why had I agreed to allow Rebecca to come with us. This was too dangerous.

Because she insisted and I couldn't tell her no.

The leader of the Atlans, an exceptionally oversized monster named Velik moved to stand in the small space separating the two pilot seats. He blocked my view of Rebecca and I nearly growled at him.

Who was the beast now?

"Have you tracked down the signal?"

"No." I checked the scanners again. "I am picking up a weak, short-range distress signal breaking through, but the frequency varies moment to moment. The signal is not consistent. Nor can I pin down an exact location."

The Atlan grunted. "The AI must be testing frequencies, trying to reach its ship." He looked down over his shoulder at my mate. "Did you place the device in a shielded location?"

"I—no. I mean, it put it in the fireproof box that's inside the safe."

"What is this safe made of?"

"I have no idea. Steel, maybe?"

"With thermal insulation?"

"It's supposed to be fireproof, and so is the box inside the safe. So, yes? Steel box inside a steel safe, lined with something so it won't burn if the center were to catch on fire."

Velik grunted. "Stroke of luck. The AI signal wouldn't be strong enough to break through. It would need to test frequencies, search for one able to penetrate your mate's safe."

"So, it's still there?" Rebecca asked.

"I believe so." Velik slapped the back of my seat. "Get us down there, Hunter. We'll take care of this. You remain here and keep your mate safe." He turned away and moved into the tiny corridor now bursting with Atlans. And weapons.

If I didn't know the Atlan beasts were giants in every possible way, I would look at those rifles and wonder what they were compensating for. In this case, no compensation was needed. These warlords simply loved to blow shit up.

Cloaking device still on, I landed the ship in the parking lot of Rebecca's youth center. The sky was dark, but this was a city. The stars were obscured by the glow of millions of artificial lights. Streetlamps illuminated most of the center's front entrance. Shadows lingered around the trees and bushes, here and there, near a doorway.

I didn't like it.

Of course, I didn't like even the idea of my mate being here.

The shudder of touchdown rocked the ship and the Atlans had the door open and were outside before I'd had a chance to turn off the propulsion system.

Next to me, Rebecca unbuckled and scooted closer to the images on the screen in front of her. The Atlans moved like liquid, flowing toward the entrance. Seconds later they had disappeared inside. Her knee bobbed up and down in a rapid movement that distracted me from my ongoing scans.

"I hope they remember the combination. He didn't write it down. Why didn't he write it down?" Rebecca's leg moved even faster. She added rocking her torso forward and back to her repertoire, one hand rubbing the spot on her lower ribs where she'd been shot, as if the site pained her. I doubted she was even aware of the action.

"Rebecca, be calm. Atlans are very good fighters. I doubt there is an army on this planet that could defeat those warlords." I reached over and placed my hand on her bouncing knee. The movement stopped at once. Thank the gods. She was going to make *me* nervous with her explosion of energy.

I wanted to be inside the building. I wanted to be out there, hunting the Siren scum who had nearly killed my mate.

Even more, I needed to be next to her, keeping her safe.

"Okay." She leaned back into the seat and closed her eyes. "Okay. But I can't watch this screen. I just can't." She rose from her seat and moved toward the now empty corridor. "I'll go get Lilah some food." She glanced down at her pet, love shining in her eyes as she leaned low and rested her forehead against the dog's. "You're probably thirsty, too. Aren't you girl?"

Lilah panted happily and followed my mate into the corridor. Moments later I heard Rebecca cooing to that dog. Praise. Affection. Sweetness. Love words.

Fuck me. I was jealous of a dog. *Again.*

Irritated at myself for the thought, I returned my attention to the scanners tracking the AI's frequency bursts. I turned on the comms, listening to the Atlans talk to one another as they moved through the building. Found the safe. Opened it.

They had it. The AI Engram was in their possession.

There was no possible way for Rokor or his accomplice to leave this planet without it. Their ship would be useless.

Excellent. I would take Rebecca back to Warden Egara, where I knew she would be safely guarded by a complex full of Atlan warlords and Prillion warriors, ensure her comfort and finally resume my hunt.

"Lilah!" Rebecca's scream hadn't fully registered before I was out of my seat, moving toward the sound.

The dog lay in a heap in the corridor, an ion blast in her side. She was breathing, but she was badly wounded.

I was to the ramp, registering Rebecca's protests.

"Stop it! Put me down. Asshole!"

There was no response. There didn't need to be. I knew who had her.

"Rokor! Let her go!"

"Come and get her, Hunter." Cruel laughter followed the challenge, then a whimper of pain.

"No!" Rebecca screamed but I did not hear fear in her voice. I heard rage.

My brave, reckless mate. Did she not realize her life was in danger? That Rokor would as soon cut her throat as listen to her cries?

I stepped into view at the top of the ship's ramp. As expected, Rokor was staring up at me, an evil snarl on his face. He held Rebecca by her neck, nearly dangling her in the air. Only the tips of her toes touched the ground. Even that was a relief. Rokor was from Rogue 5, a Hyperion hybrid. He could rip out her throat with a flick of his wrist...or one bite from his fangs.

"What do you want, Rokor?"

"I want my AI engram."

"I don't have it."

"Lies." He shook Rebecca enough to make her feet swing in mid-air. Her fingers were curled around his grip like claws. "Come now, Hunter. Stop hiding in your ship. We picked up the AI's frequency coming from here. Give me what I want, and I'll give you what you want."

"Stark! No! There are two more. It's a trap!"

Of course it was a trap. It was always a trap. "Where is your friend, Rokor? Or did you kill him, too?"

"He was useless."

"And you didn't want to share." There were too many humans on this planet Rokor could sell his drugs to. Weak. Small. Rokor could have been a king on Earth. A god.

I'd been sent by the Coalition to bring him to justice. I would have done my job. But now he'd dared touch my mate. Hurt her. Nearly killed her.

For that alone he would die.

I was an Elite Hunter. Rebecca had never seen me track my prey. Never seen me kill. I had no desire to show her that side of myself, but I had no choice.

Calling upon my ancient bloodline, I allowed my cells to fill with power. Intention. Stillness.

One moment I stood at the top of the ship's ramp. The next I sliced Rokor's arm from his body, the detached limb still attached to Rebecca's neck.

Turning, I shoved a blade into Rokor's heart with one hand and pulled Rebecca into place behind me with the other. I now stood between Rebecca and the other attackers.

Pity. They were human.

Rebecca shouted as she pulled the hand from her neck and threw Rokor's limb as far away as she could manage. "Ugh! Gross. Oh my god! You cut off his arm."

I did not have time to comfort her. The human males were armed as well. Their weapons made of metal and stinking of oil. I knew they were ancient projectile firearms. Not a threat to me, but to Rebecca? Lethal.

Moving faster than I ever had in my life, my vision blurred as I sliced each man's throat in turn. Rebecca wobbled from the loss of my arm around her, but I was back at her side before she could fall.

"What?" Her eyes grew round with shock as she watched the human men reach for their throats one by one. Blood spurted from their necks. Confusion clouded their gazes. They both crumpled to the ground to bleed out.

I scanned our surroundings for further threats and found none. Pulling her into my arms, I held her close. Stroked her back as she shuddered. "There's that word again, mate."

A faint laugh from her allowed me to breathe again. "You saved my life. Again."

Relief made my knees weak, relief that she did not pull away from me, did not fear me. I had killed in front of her and still she clung to me. "Are you afraid of me?"

"What?"

Gods be damned, I was going to ban that word from her vocabulary.

Slowly, I placed my hands on either side of her face and tilted her head up so I could look into her eyes. "Are you afraid of me?"

She looked confused. "Why would I be afraid of you?"

"I did what I had to do to protect you. I wish you had not been forced to see me like that."

She lifted her hands and placed them over mine, locking my palms to her soft cheeks. "They were evil, Stark. Pure evil. I'm glad you killed them." Tears gathered in her eyes and an ache built inside my chest. "I'm sorry you have to do that. Kill, I mean, to protect other people. It must be horrible for you."

I had sliced open three men's throats in front of her and she was worried about me?

I kissed her. There was nothing else I could do. She made no sense, my female. None.

Thank the gods.

I heard the Atlans exit the building. Velik whistled slowly as he inspected the scene, the others fanning out behind him. "Didn't leave anything for the rest of us, eh?"

"No."

He nodded. "Didn't know what they were dealing with, did they?"

"No."

"Scary fuckers." He tilted his head at his fellow warlords. "Let's get out of here."

"Two are human, but that one is from Rogue 5."

"Got it." With a slight nod from Velik, two of his men moved to pick up Rokor's corpse.

Holding onto my mate with one hand, I dug in my uniform pocket with the other and tossed the DNA scanner as well as a bioflare to one of the Atlans. He caught it in midair and grinned.

"Always wanted to use one of these things."

"Well, get on with it." I lifted Rebecca and cradled her in my arms. This time she was not gravely injured. This time she wrapped her arms around my neck and rested her head on my shoulder.

She sniffled. Shuddered.

"What is wrong? Are you in pain?"

"He killed Lilah." Her words were broken.

"No, love. Your golden beast is alive. Injured, but alive. I promise you."

The news seemed to break the tight control she had on her emotions. She trembled as I carried her to the safety of my ship. Together we knelt beside Lilah. The valiant dog managed to lift her head and offer her mistress a kiss in the form of a swipe of her enormous tongue on Rebecca's wrist.

She would live.

I paid no attention to the Atlans, looking away from my mate only when one of them appeared at my side with a ReGen wand. I lifted the device to Rebecca's neck. She tried to shove my hands away.

"Lilah needs it more than I do."

I grabbed both of her hands in one of mine and waited for her to look at me. Our gazes locked. "You will always come first, Rebecca. Always."

She lowered her eyelids for long seconds. I expected an argument.

When her eyes opened I saw something there I had never seen before. I didn't dare hope.

Then she said the words.

"I love you, Stark. Thank you for taking care of me."

"I love you, Rebecca. If you will have me, I'd like to take care of you for the rest of our lives."

"Forever?"

"Yes."

"On Everis?"

"Yes."

"Can Lilah come?"

"Of course."

The Atlans moved around us, taking care of the ship and their weapons. Rokor's body had been incinerated. The ship lifted from the ground and still I did not move. One of them handed the DNA tracer back to me and I shoved it in my pocket without looking. I couldn't take my eyes from Rebecca. Needed her answer.

"Yes. I want to be with you." She leaned back and exposed her neck, trusting me to heal her, to take care of her.

To love her.

Always.

"Okay."

A SPECIAL THANK YOU TO MY READERS...

Want more? I've got *hidden* bonus content on my web site *exclusively* for those on my mailing list.

If you are already on my email list, you don't need to do a thing! Simply scroll to the bottom of my newsletter emails and click on the *super-secret* link.

Not a member? What are you waiting for? In addition to bonus content (great new stuff will be added regularly) you will always be in the loop - you'll never have to wonder when my newest release will hit the stores—AND you will get a free book as a special welcome gift.

Sign up now! http://freescifiromance.com

FIND YOUR INTERSTELLAR MATCH!

YOUR mate is out there. Take the test today and discover your perfect match. Are you ready for a sexy alien mate (or two)?

VOLUNTEER NOW!

interstellarbridesprogram.com

DO YOU LOVE AUDIOBOOKS?

Grace Goodwin's books are now available as audiobooks...everywhere.

LET'S TALK!

Interested in joining my **Sci-Fi Squad**? Meet new like-minded sci-fi romance fanatics and chat with Grace! Be part of a private Facebook group that shares pictures and fun news! Join here:

https://www.facebook.com/groups/scifisquad/

Want to talk about Grace Goodwin books with others? Join the **SPOILER ROOM** and spoil away! Your GG BFFs are waiting! (And so is Grace) Join here:

https://www.facebook.com/groups/ggspoilerroom/

GET A FREE BOOK!

JOIN MY MAILING LIST TO BE THE FIRST TO KNOW OF NEW RELEASES, FREE BOOKS, SPECIAL PRICES AND OTHER AUTHOR GIVEAWAYS.

http://freescifiromance.com

ALSO BY GRACE GOODWIN

Interstellar Brides® Program

Assigned a Mate

Mated to the Warriors

Claimed by Her Mates

Taken by Her Mates

Mated to the Beast

Mastered by Her Mates

Tamed by the Beast

Mated to the Vikens

Her Mate's Secret Baby

Mating Fever

Her Viken Mates

Fighting For Their Mate

Her Rogue Mates

Claimed By The Vikens

The Commanders' Mate

Matched and Mated

Hunted

Viken Command

The Rebel and the Rogue

Rebel Mate

Surprise Mates

Rogue Enforcer

Chosen by the Vikens

Marked Mate

Interstellar Brides® Program Boxed Set - Books 6-8

Interstellar Brides® Program Boxed Set - Books 9-12

Interstellar Brides® Program Boxed Set - Books 13-16

Interstellar Brides® Program Boxed Set - Books 17-20

Interstellar Brides® Program Boxed Set - Books 21-24

Bad Boys of Rogue 5

Interstellar Brides® Program: The Colony

Surrender to the Cyborgs

Mated to the Cyborgs

Cyborg Seduction

Her Cyborg Beast

Cyborg Fever

Rogue Cyborg

Cyborg's Secret Baby

Her Cyborg Warriors

Claimed by the Cyborgs

The Colony Boxed Set 1

The Colony Boxed Set 2

The Colony Boxed Set 3

Interstellar Brides® Program: The Virgins

The Alien's Mate

His Virgin Mate

Claiming His Virgin

His Virgin Bride

His Virgin Princess

The Virgins - Complete Boxed Set

Interstellar Brides® Program: Ascension Saga

Ascension Saga, book 1

Ascension Saga, book 2

Ascension Saga, book 3

Trinity: Ascension Saga - Volume 1

Ascension Saga, book 4

Ascension Saga, book 5

Ascension Saga, book 6

Faith: Ascension Saga - Volume 2

Ascension Saga, book 7

Ascension Saga, book 8

Ascension Saga, book 9

Destiny: Ascension Saga - Volume 3

Interstellar Brides® Program: The Beasts

Bachelor Beast

Maid for the Beast

Beauty and the Beast

The Beasts Boxed Set - Books 1-3

Big Bad Beast

Beast Charming

Bargain with a Beast

The Beasts Boxed Set - Books 4-6

Beast's Secret Baby

Starfighter Training Academy

The First Starfighter

Starfighter Command

Elite Starfighter

Starfighter Training Academy Boxed Set

Other Books

Dragon Chains

Their Conquered Bride

Wild Wolf Claiming: A Howl's Romance

SUBSCRIBE TODAY!

Hi there! Grace Goodwin here. I am SO excited to invite you into my intense, crazy, sexy, romantic, imagination and the worlds born as a result. From Battlegroup Karter to The Colony and on behalf of the entire Coalition Fleet of Planets, I welcome you! Visit my Patreon page for additional bonus content, sneak peaks, and insider information on upcoming books as well as the opportunity to receive NEW RELEASE BOOKS before anyone else! See you there! ~ Grace

Grace's PATREON: https://www.patreon.com/gracegoodwin

ABOUT GRACE

Grace Goodwin is a USA Today and international bestselling author of Sci-Fi and Paranormal romance with over a million books sold. Grace's titles are available worldwide on all retailers, in multiple languages, and in ebook, print, audio and other reading App formats.

Grace is a full-time writer whose earliest movie memories are of Luke Skywalker, Han Solo, and real, working light sabers. (Still waiting for Santa to come through on that one.) Now Grace writes sexy-as-hell sci-fi romance six days a week. In her spare time, she reads, watches campy sci-fi and enjoys spending time with family and friends. No matter where she is, there is always a part of her dreaming up new worlds and exciting characters for her next book.

Grace loves to chat with readers and can frequently be found lurking in her Facebook groups. Interested in joining her **Sci-Fi Squad**? Meet new like-minded sci-fi romance fanatics and chat with Grace! Join here: https://www.facebook.com/groups/scifisquad/

Want to talk about Grace Goodwin books with others? Join the **SPOILER ROOM** and spoil away! Your GG BFFs are waiting! (And so is Grace) Join here:

https://www.facebook.com/groups/ggspoilerroom/

www.ingramcontent.com/pod-product-compliance
Lightning Source LLC
LaVergne TN
LVHW011848060526
838200LV00054B/4232